What I Believe

written by
Jennifer Murphy-Morrical

illustrated by
Sue Shanahan

BEYOND WORDS
PUBLISHING

*To Hunter and Elle, who inspire me; Steve, who loves and supports me;
and Amie, who always believed.—J. M.*

For my children, who gave my heart wings.—S. S.

Published by
Beyond Words Publishing, Inc.
20827 NW Cornell Road, Suite 500
Hillsboro, Oregon 97124
503-531-8700

Editors: Barbara Leese and Kristin Hilton
Cover and interior design: Jerry Soga

Printed in Korea
Distributed to the book trade by Publishers Group West

ISBN: 1-58270-122-9

The corporate mission of Beyond Words Publishing, Inc:
Inspire to Integrity

What do you believe?

I believe that when doors shut, windows open.

I believe spring brings out hope in all of us.

I believe your special talents will light up the world.

I believe play is an important part of every day.

I believe dreams help you discover yourself.

I believe faeries dance at sunrise and sunset and in the moonlight.

I believe animals know more than we think they do.

I believe being able to receive from others is just as important as giving.

I believe your guardian angel
never leaves your side.

I believe a good friend is a treasure, and you need to take care of your treasure.

I believe if you need a nap,
you should take one.

I believe music and dance
fill your spirit.

I believe life can give you the best you can imagine.

What I believe in the most
is you—
who you are, who you will
be, and how you will
give your special talents
to the world.

Share Your Beliefs

Dear ....

I believe . . .

You are special because . . .

I love you, ...

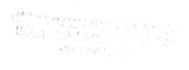